The Terror At
LOVE LAKE

Joey Powell

MADAXEMEDIA.COM

Print ISBN: 979-8-9891730-8-2
EBook ISBN: 979-8-9891730-9-9

Book Cover by Joey Powell

A few things before we start ...

Hi there. I'm the Owner & Operator of Mad Axe Media, a publisher of dark genre fiction and 90s nostalgia horror. I'm also the writer of the short piece you're about to read, as well as the author of the novel *Nightmares From the Gray* and the forthcoming novella *Squirming All the Way Up* (2025).

I've included at the end of this chapbook a guide to all of the upcoming publications from Mad Axe Media through the end of 2025. If you're into dark and twisted stories, flip over to learn about *Hiding Lies* by Stephanie Rose. Interested in the dangers of tech? *JK-LOL* by Patrick Barb is for you. Is religious horror your thing? J.V. Gachs has you covered with *Unholy*. And if you're into serial killer psychology, prepare yourself for *Son of a Serial Killer* by Andrew Adams.

On the lighter side, we have five upcoming titles in the Totally Freaked! line of books, each involving standalone stories of YA 90s nostalgia horror that pay homage to such greats as Stine and Pike.

I truly hope you're as excited to read these works as I am to share them with the world.

I'd like to thank Tiffany Koplin from Indie Book Boxes and Books of Horror for being an all-around amazing ambassador for indie horror fiction. She's the hero we need, though I'm not sure we deserve.

Thank you to Isaac Nightingale and Julie Hiner for

beta reading *The Terror at Love Lake*. They're both incredible horror authors and I'm lucky to be both a fan and a friend of each.

I would also like to thank the Internet for confirming that pepper spray was made with flammable liquid in the 80s. You'll understand soon enough ...

And thank you, the reader, for reading. Give me a shout of Instagram @wowcooljoeywrites if you'd like.

-Joey Powell
Owner & Operator of Mad Axe Media

PRESENT DAY

Freaky Local Legends Podcasts:

The Blood Moon Murders

(Transcript)

Hello, freaks. This is Donny Roth, and you're listening to the Freaky Local Legends podcast, where we break down the most gruesome, insane, and unexplainable things that have happened in the most unexpected places.

Today's episode is very near and dear to my heart as it details an event that occured right here in my backyard. Today we are talking about the Blood Moon Murders at Love Lake.

Quite the oxymoron, indeed.

The year is 1981. We're at the tail end of summer in Echo Ridge, a quaint rural town located in the heart of North Carolina. A place with a large body of water on the

outskirts of town, surrounded by
lake houses only the old money fami-
lies could afford. Since they often
remained vacant, teens would find
their way into the small community
and, well … do what teenagers do.

But there was no love at Love Lake
on this night. Instead, there was a
murder, evidence of a ritual, and a
mysterious unidentified man.

Today, we're going to do a deep
dive and try to find some answers
based on what was found at the crime
scene, as well as the disturbing
eyewitness testimony from the sole
survivor herself: real-life final
girl Diane Doakes.

If you know anything about this
story, you've likely heard the theory that Miss Doakes was behind
everything. Yes, she was found with
the blood of the victims all over
her cheerleading uniform, but look
no further than the lacerations on
the victims' skin, cuts that exam-
iners determined were from multiple
weapons: an ax, a switchblade, and

a hatchet. The axe was left in the front yard of the house in which the murders took place, wedged in the skull of Lloyd McGinty. The switchblade was stuck in Lloyd's chest as well. The hatchet was in the back of young Wendy Gibbs, who lost both her eyes in the carnage and would die a few weeks later under very unusual circumstances.

Also consider the condition in which McGinty, Diane's boyfriend at the time, was found. One of his arms and both of his legs bent in ways God never intended. Now, all you listeners know I'm a feminist, but … I just have to state the obvious. It would be very difficult for someone of Diane's stature to overpower football player Lloyd McGinty and force his limbs backward.

Today, we're going over Diane's original testimony made available online thanks to a leak from the Echo Ridge police department, and, folks, this is a *very* strange story. Diane's statement involves an im-possibly large man killing Lloyd and the other victims, a magic switch that cast a forcefield around the property, trapping them inside, and worms.

That's right … Worms.

Was it possible she lured the victims there, killed them, and suffered a psychotic break? But then how would anyone explain the many sightings of the so-called Echo Ridge Giant since then? A shared delusion of a paranoid public? A phony local legend passed around by bored children to scare each other?

Is Diane Doakes innocent? Is the Giant really out there, ready to strike again? One thing's for sure:

What happened that night at Love Lake is likely stranger than any theory you or I could imagine.

August 19th,
1981

D iane Doakes told herself she wasn't, under any circumstances, going to Love Lake tonight.

Warm August air surrounded her as she stood outside the gates of the high school football stadium, watching hordes of attendees exit.

A victory for the Echo Ridge Rebels to start the season.

She despised having to go through all this again. The stiff fabric of her cheerleading uniform—an ugly combination of gray with red accents—chafed her tailbone with every step. Her wrists ached from several handsprings, both front and back. Not only did she have to stand and twirl through two and half hours of a football game she could barely see over the helmets of benchwarmers, but the dread of the eventual conversation she would have with her boyfriend, Lloyd McGinty, also weighed on her, strumming her brain like the hands of a ticking clock.

It was a conversation they had to have *now*, before Lloyd had a chance to drive her to Love Lake. After all, she was not, under any circumstances, going to Love Lake tonight.

Diane liked Lloyd just fine. But did she lust for him? In the four weeks they'd spent together over the summer, she pondered the question quite a bit. More than was normal for most girls lucky enough to catch his eye, she assumed. She was seventeen, and, as several chats with her girlfriends assured her, should have been *very* interested in sex, but she just... wasn't. The thought of seeing Lloyd with his clothes off, that rock-hard appendage hanging from the middle of his body like a flag post, was more comical than erotic to Diane. And when Lloyd drove her to an abandoned construction site earlier that week, those feelings were confirmed.

Lloyd had *wanted* sex that night. He made it clear almost immediately, asking if they could "make love" in a way that made Diane gag. But Diane's denial of his advances triggered something in Lloyd. Gone was the sweet, romantic boy she thought she knew, instead replaced by a being of pure testosterone and masculine rage. He'd grabbed her coat in an attempt to "help her take it off," but she slapped him away.

He ended up apologizing several times over. "I'm so ashamed," he told Diane in a way that saddened her deeply. This was the hold he had on her. She didn't lust for him, nor did she love him, but she cared for him.

"Are you still coming to the lake with me?" he'd asked. "It'll just be a few buddies from another school. I—I know the lake has a reputation, but... we're just gonna party. I swear."

Yes, Love Lake had a reputation, indeed.

His apologies didn't help stave off Diane's dream that night of Lloyd with an impossibly wide smile, the sharp teeth of a piranha, and bloodshot eyes, clawing at her skin as she tried to leave the car. They were both stuck in a slow-moving purgatory—her trying to open the door, his jagged nails digging holes in her skin, scraping through flesh and dragging across her spine.

And so, on the night of the first game of the season, she decided she had to break things off. The same night on which the local weatherman had announced a blood moon in advance, so called because the moon would be eclipsed and illuminated by the sunlight refracted by the earth's atmosphere, casting a red glow over Echo Ridge.

How fitting.

She told herself she wasn't going to Love Lake. Under no circumstances would she allow herself to be pulled into that puppy-dog stare, the same look he gave her when he said he was embarrassed by the way he'd acted that night.

Finally, Lloyd came out of the locker room, his thick brown hair wet and stiff from a shower, wearing a t-shirt with the sleeves cut off, his round shoulders and biceps sprouting outward like mushrooms. Many girls found Lloyd's muscle-bound aesthetic exciting. He would easily find another one to seduce.

Lloyd's football buddies crawled out of the locker room behind him, laughing and basking in the glory of a win. All eyes fell on Diane. The guys nudged Lloyd, cackling like children.

"Twelve yards away from the single-game school rushing record," a deep voice split through the crowd noise from Diane's side, worming its way into her ear. She turned to face a large, towering kid in an Echo Ridge Football T-shirt. The August heat hadn't been good to him, judging by the ring of sweat blooming from his shirt collar. "You keep putting out and maybe he'll get that extra twelve yards next game." The boy smirked.

It took a moment for Diane to process what the sweaty boy had said. By the time she had, the boy had walked away, perfectly comfortable with the assertion that Diane's subservient sexual satisfaction to a kid who runs fast would lead to him running faster.

It was no use correcting him anyway—or telling him that Lloyd's stiff dick seemed less like an instrument of pleasure and more like a knife for which to stab her with.

Lloyd approached Diane, leaving his entourage behind him, and flashed a smile before placing a dry kiss on Diane's lips. She wanted to recoil, but attendees were still filing out of the gates, and doing so would embarrass both of them.

Lloyd beamed. "I was so close to the record. I

thought about you the entire game. I wanted to get it for you."

He was deliriously happy. Manic in a way Diane had never been. A breath dragged from her lips, and the words she'd intended for him stayed buried in her throat.

Sensing Diane's indifference, Lloyd shrugged. "Number two on the chart isn't so bad though."

While the voice inside her head screamed what she wanted to say ("I was hoping we could talk!"), instead, what came out was, "I'm so proud of you."

"You ready to celebrate?" he asked. "Arthur's gonna be waiting on us."

Under no circumstances am I going to Love Lake, she reminded herself.

But she couldn't bring herself to shatter his moment of bliss.

S he was going to Love Lake.

Dammit.

Lloyd held one hand on the wheel, the other hovering over Diane's limp hand. Time and again, she caught him in her periphery stealing glances, becoming increasingly aware of his paranoia that *something* was wrong.

Something was, most definitely, wrong. Diane had never hidden her feelings well. No volume of Stevie Nicks throbbing out of Lloyd's busted radio could fill the silence between them.

"You're quiet tonight," Lloyd said finally. "Tired from the game?"

"Yeah," she answered quickly. "It was a fun game to watch."

Lloyd snickered. He knew she hated football. He was even one of the few people who knew she hated cheerleading—that she only did it because her parents told her that being a part of a team would give her a leg up on her college applications. She wished she never told him that.

Lloyd stopped snickering and gave her another glance. "Is this about the other night?" Lloyd asked.

Diane didn't answer. As soon as the question settled in her consciousness, she realized how dark the road was, only lit by twin orbs of dim headlights. The trees surrounding them would have perhaps been calming in the daytime, but they carried the shapes of angry claws reaching out for the vehicle—for Diane. The question hit her chest like a brick, and she suddenly realized how isolated they were. The memories of the abandoned construction site and her nightmare congealed, and she forced herself to look at Lloyd simply to not imagine his demonic alter ego from the nightmare.

"No, just ... exhausted," she replied, subtly thumbing the small canister of pepper spray she'd clipped to the inside of her hip.

"I already apologized for that," Lloyd said.

"I know. I'm not mad."

"You don't realize what you do to me. You're just... so..." His face widened with a smile, possibly thinking his words were some form of flattery. "We don't have to. Not until you're ready."

"Did you tell all your friends we *did*?"

His face drooped stupidly. "No, of course not. People talk, Die. I can't control what they say."

She hated that shorthand. How could he think the word "Die" was a good pet name?

"I'm not asking what *other* people talk about. I just want to know if you told anyone that we…" She nodded. "… you know."

Lloyd searched for an answer. All the while, a goofy, "Uhhhh," slipped out of his mouth.

It was all the answer she needed. Diane clenched her teeth. "That's just killer, Lloyd. Really, just… bitchin'."

"I mean, I didn't… Come on, Die, it's a locker room. Guys talk about stuff."

"So your whole football team thinks I put out?"

"I didn't say anything. I just… didn't say we… *didn't* do anything."

Diane wanted to be anywhere but inside that car, stuck with him.

"It's not a big deal, Die," Lloyd said. "It's not like we weren't going to do it eventually."

Her stomach churned as something inside of it tried to force its way up her throat. "Oh my god. No we fucking weren't."

Lloyd went silent. Not ashamed-silent or embarrassed-silent. This was angry silence. His jaw tightened. The rubber of the steering wheel grunted under his grip.

"Can you just take me home?" Diane said.

Lloyd took a moment, clamping his teeth, his eyes narrow and fierce. "We're going to the party," he said. "We can cool off and talk about this later."

Stevie Nicks had faded from the stereo, and some band Diane didn't know replaced her with a jovial tune. It couldn't quell the knot in her stomach. No longer was it disgust for Lloyd.

It was fear.

L loyd came to a stop and *ripped* the emergency brake, which served no purpose, since they were on flat land. She chalked it up to pent-up male aggression—some biological urge to lift, throw, or rip something when a guy doesn't get his way.

"We're gonna have a good time tonight," Lloyd said sternly before turning to Diane. "Right?"

"Right," Diane answered, thumbing the can of pepper spray again just to assure herself it was still there. She wouldn't have to use it.

No, she *definitely* wouldn't have to use it.

She just had to get through the night, avoid him the rest of the weekend, and break things off next week.

Diane opened her door and put a sneaker on the gravel beneath Lloyd's vehicle. In an instant, the mosquitoes were on her, zipping, pecking, fiending for blood. She slapped her leg to clear it of whatever was stinging it and stood, lightly closing the door behind her.

The narrow driveway was blocked by three other cars and split in two—on the right side was the entrance to the lake house, and on the left side was a downhill slope leading to the boathouse, which sat right on the edge of the lake.

Diane Doakes had officially arrived at Love Lake.

While the lake house was a three-story behemoth the likes of which Diane's family would never be able to afford, the boathouse was nearly the size of Diane's ranch-style home, forcing her to wonder just how big the damn boat was inside of it.

"Whose house is this?" Diane asked.

Lloyd stepped out of the driver's side. "I told you. Arthur Dodson."

"And you know him how?"

"Met him at a party last weekend. Said he'd have the house to himself tonight." Lloyd circled around the hood of the car and gave Diane a weak smile. "We're good... Right?" He held out his hand.

Diane shot back a smile weaker than his and met his calloused hand with hers.

Together they made the short walk up to the entrance. The moonlight cast daggers across the gentle ripples of the lake. Diane expected there to be music, singing, clanking of bottles, all muffled within the lake house, but instead, there was nothing. Not even lamplight seeping out through the blinds or a porch light to guide their steps.

There was only the calm movement of the lake.

As if he'd heard her thoughts, Lloyd muttered, "Where is everyone? Did they go skinny dipping or somethin'?"

They took the three small steps up the porch. Lloyd noticed the crack in the door before Diane. "That's weird. The door's open."

But all Diane could focus on was the dark stain on the outside of the doorframe, right around where the knob would have been, were it not slightly ajar. She followed the stain with her eyes as best she could in the moonglow, scanning from the frame down to the threshold and past the steps.

Lloyd chuckled. "Looks like someone spilled their beer."

Idiot.

The unmistakable stench of beer would have hit them as soon as they took the first step.

Diane reached out and dabbed the stain on the doorframe, then brought it to her nose, taking a whiff of something stale and metallic.

"It's blood," she said.

"Uh ... Are you sure?" Lloyd responded.

"I'm pretty damn sure what blood smells like, Lloyd. We're leaving." She turned and he caught her wrist.

"Hang on," Lloyd said. "I'm sure everything's fine."

Just as she was about to threaten to remove Lloyd's hand from his wrist, the door opened. "Leaving?" the voice behind the door said. The candle flame danced on the figure's back, outlining him in a jittery orange glow. Diane could barely make out a single feature in his face, but the shakiness in his voice was unmistakable. "But you just got here. And uh … a little late by my count."

"Arthur!" Lloyd exclaimed, throwing up his hands for a stiff high five. The boy named Arthur threw his hand out, and the two boys met in a loud *smack*. "Sorry, just celebrating a victory with the boys."

"The rushing record, right?" Arthur said. "Or close to it?"

Lloyd giggled, basking in the praise. "News travels fast, I guess."

"What happened here?" Diane interrupted.

"Uh …" Arthur's voice wobbled once again.

"My girl's a little freaked out by all this on the porch," Lloyd said. "Thinks it's blood or somethin'."

"Oh … that… um…" Arthur stammered.

Diane could barely track the mystery boy's eyes, but she could swear she saw a glimmer of them glancing toward the boathouse.

"Yeah, I gotta get that cleaned up," Arthur said. "Just an accident. Why don't you guys come in?"

"Where's everybody else?" Diane asked.

"Don't be rude, babe," Lloyd said, walking over the threshold with an arm on Diane's shoulder.

She shrugged it away as subtly as she could, taking one look back at the boathouse. The moon hovered above it in a burst of white light, reminding her that soon, everything would be caked in red.

"They went out to grab some booze," Arthur said from inside the house. "They'll be back soon."

Classic and old-fashioned paneling lined the walls of the living room. Gaudy, plumb furniture filled the interior in clouds of dust that tickled Diane's nose. She sneezed from the collection of free-flowing particles, then nearly gagged from a putrid stench.

"Yo, Arthur, what is that smell, dude?" Lloyd said, masking his nose with a forearm.

"Oh, someone got sick and … threw up," Arthur said unconfidently. When he turned to them, Diane finally got a good look at him. A redhead with thick sideburns and a jean jacket. His eyes were surrounded by dark circles, giving his eyes a sunken effect. He looked like he hadn't slept in days.

"Too much beer?" Lloyd asked.

"Yeah."

But the others were going out to get booze. Something didn't sit right with Diane. Everything felt off, from the candles to the quietness to Arthur squirming like a sex addict in church. And that smell …

Something was *dead* in this house.

"You guys make yourselves comfortable," Arthur said. "I'm gonna go check the breaker box. Should be able to get the lights back on soon."

"Where the fuckin' music!" Lloyd said. "Let's get this party started!"

"The boombox runs on electricity, Lloyd," Arthur said. "I'm gonna try to fix it."

Lloyd sighed. "Alright. I guess we'll just … wait up,

then."

But Diane had no intention of waiting. As soon as Arthur disappeared behind the basement door, Diane began her fast walk out of the house.

"Babe, where you goin'?" Lloyd said.

"This isn't right. Take me home."

"Babe, come on!"

Diane stood in front of the door and turned. "Take me home *now*, Lloyd."

"Don't be such a buzzkill. Look," Lloyd took a deep breath. "I know you're *still* upset about the other night. I know you don't think my apology was good enough, but... it's not my fault, you know."

"What's not your fault?"

"You're a tease. I see the way you move out on the field. You *want* people to notice. I noticed. Maybe I got the wrong idea."

Diane turned to face him. "It's cheerleading, Lloyd. I'm not out there stripping."

"They know what they're doin', putting you in that outfit."

"Who knows what they're—Lloyd, it's a goddamn cheerleading outfit. Do you know how uncomfortable this thing is?"

"Take it off and maybe you won't be so... *uncomfortable.*" Lloyd giggled, becoming more and more childish by the second.

His smile quickly faded. "That was a joke. Come on, Die. Lighten up."

"Stop calling me that."

"What's got your panties in a wad? You should be so lucky to date me," Lloyd said, approaching her quickly, blurring the lines between his true form and the demonic version from her nightmare. He grabbed her wrist. "I don't know if you saw what I did out there tonight, but I just rushed for one hundred ninety-four yards. Twelve—"

"Yeah, twelve yards away from the record. I don't give a fuck. Get your hand off me."

Lloyd tightened his grip. "I'm not gonna let you ruin the night for everyone. For me."

With her free arm, Diane clutched the canister of pepper spray, slightly larger than a tube of lipstick in her palm. She whipped it out, aimed the nozzle at Lloyd's eyes, and pressed down hard.

Lloyd swatted her wrist, diverting the spray successfully.

The canister fell onto the hardwoods.

"Pepper spray?! Really?! With all these open flames? My cousin caught fire messin' with that stuff! How *dare* you?!" Lloyd shoved her hard, forcing her off her feet and onto her back with a hard *thud*.

Diane's elbow caught the bulk of the impact. It'd be sore the next day, but she was fine.

"Diane, I ..." Lloyd held up his hands as if considering coming to her aid, but his widened eyes quickly came back down to normal. "Fuckin' pepper spray. Is that really what you think of me? Whatever. I'm gonna go help Arthur with the breaker box. Walk the fuck home if you want to. And take your dinky lit spray can with you."

Lloyd kicked the pepper spray over to Diane, then walked over to the basement door and opened it, following Arthur down.

Diane grunted and lifted herself up, then grabbed the pepper spray and clipped it back to the inside of her skirt for safekeeping. She pulled open the front door, hoping she could find a way out of Love Lake. Surely one of the neighbors had a phone she could use.

But something was very wrong with the outside of the house as well.

A sheet of floating, translucent film surrounded the property, wrapping around the boathouse, behind Lloyd's car, and around the backside of the house, fading into the sky. The thin consistency was almost like a bubble before it popped, Diane thought, with light refracting through it and reflecting off of it.

Whatever the hell it was, it wasn't there when they came in. It was as if a button had been pressed the minute they walked into the house to raise the near-invisible gates, which faded into the sky, right below the beginnings of the blood moon.

With her surroundings smothered in a pale red, Diane called out for the one person she didn't want to be around. "Lloyd?"

A scream answered her, but not from Lloyd.

From the boathouse.

One of the wooden double doors flew open. A girl with long brown hair, matted down by something—Was that *blood?*—on one side of her head sprung loose from the structure. The stretched collar of her sweater bobbed with each frantic step. "Help!" she yelled. "Help!"

Her eyes locked with Diane's—one eye, to be more specific. The other eye was covered up with something.

"Help! He's gonna kill us!"

"Lloyd!" Diane yelled louder this time.

As the girl came closer, Diane realized her eye wasn't covered.

It was gone, and in its place, a red, hollow pit oozed blood.

"Ohmygodjesuschristwhathappened," Diane said quickly, holding a breath in her chest as the girl came closer.

She was nearly ten yards away when—

Thwack.

The girl fell to the ground with the handle of a hatchet sticking out from her spine.

Behind her, a figure stood outside the boathouse, lowering his arm. In the pale red glow of the blood moon, Diane saw all of him.

It was the largest man Diane had ever seen—maybe seven feet tall—with mythically wide shoulders that sat below what looked like a clay mask on his head. His clothes were stitched together haphazardly, a quilt of random fabrics with no uniformity—the tattered collage of a madman. He moved one heavy foot forward as the girl with one eye writhed on the ground, her spine failing to allow her arms to push her up.

Frozen in place, all Diane could do was scream.

"Lloyd!"

Something hard like a boulder knocked Diane off balance. She spun on the ground to see Lloyd climbing to his feet with a bloody gash in his stomach, painting his prized letterman jacket red.

"That dickweed tried to kill me!" Lloyd said. His eyes fell on the translucent wall around them, the dying girl, the madman, processing every impossible detail at once. "What the hell is going on?"

"We should have never come here," Diane said, getting her feet under her, ready to sprint.

Flick. Lloyd opened his switchblade, eyes fixed on the slowly approaching madman. Diane had heard that switchblade open several times when they were sitting around with his group of friends, with Lloyd boasting that he just *wished* someone would mess with him. "After all, I gotta protect my girl," he would say, grinning in that lustful way Diane had come to recognize.

He finally had his opportunity to do just that now.

"Hey! What the hell did you do to this girl?!"

"Lloyd ... We need to go to the car *now*."

The madman continued his slow approach, and the closer he came, the larger he appeared.

"I'll fuck you up, man!" Lloyd yelled. "Your boy Arthur in there? Things didn't turn out so well for him."

"Lloyd!"

The giant picked up his pace, moving quicker than his size should have allowed.

Diane turned and ran in the direction the man

wasn't—into the driveway, straight past the line of cars.

Her feet mashed against the gravel.

Gravel soon became dirt.

A few more steps and she'd be through the floating gate that had only just appeared at the end of the driveway. Was it some trick of the light?

She'd know soon enough.

"Wait! No! No! N—!" Lloyd's screams from behind Diane were silenced like an ejected cassette tape.

She held her hand up to meet the translucent, soapy surface first, just in case it was more solid than it appeared. It went straight through, and the rest of her body followed.

Everything went dark.

Though she couldn't comprehend it, she fell head-first into a shapeless void. With ground having disappeared under her feet, she pedaled against nothing.

Streaks of light—reds, yellows, blues—flew past her, or maybe *she* flew past *them*—balls of gaseous matter, isolated space, untethered to anything she could see. A cluster of stars that would have otherwise been beautiful had she not been ripped out of everything she understood to be time and spot.

She was falling...

Down...

Down...

Down...

Until she stopped.

No longer was she weightless. The force of gravity pinned her body to a cement floor. The stench of old, rotted wood swarmed her nostrils.

"You ... You can't leave ... "

That voice ...

"They won't let you leave ... I'm ... I'm so sorry."

Arthur's voice.

But he was in the basement.

Diane blinked Arthur into existence—his nose smashed and bleeding, his left eye swollen. The result of his tussle with Lloyd—the one that "didn't turn out so well" for him.

Dark floorboards hung high above his head and a rickety side staircase sat behind him, the top steps lit by a single overhead bulb.

She *was* in the basement.

"I'm sorry. I-I didn't know any of this was gonna happen. They just gave me an envelope of money and said to bring four kids here so they could do some ritual. I didn't know anyone was gonna die. You have to believe me. I had no idea."

A body flopped on top of Diane, suddenly appearing out of thin air.

"What the ..." It was Lloyd, panting, once again making contact with Diane. "Where ..." He rolled off of Diane.

"You can't leave," Arthur said, backing away until his back collided with the stairwell. "Not until the ritual's done."

A hum tickled Diane's eardrums, and she turned her head to the sound. There on the wall was the circuit breaker Arthur had pretended to come down and fix, but next to it was a large metal lever turned up inside a gearbox, with a large tube surging with electric energy and vanishing into the cement. Something that would be more fitting in the workshop of Victor Frankenstein than a lake house basement.

She stood and peered at the wall behind her.

But it wasn't a wall—not fully, at least. The frame of a wall encased a rectangular mass of something thin and black, wobbling in gentle waves like a liquid portrait hung slightly above the ground.

"Did we just come through that?" Diane asked.

"They told me to turn that thing on," Arthur said, pointing to the lever. "I-I don't know what's going on."

"What the hell is this place?" Lloyd asked.

But the answer was obvious to Diane.

It was a trap. And they were caught in it.

"Who's 'they'?" Lloyd pressed again.

"I-I don't know. Some rich family," Arthur replied. "They said they owed a debt to the ancient ones. That the ancient ones, they … they just want to *feel*."

Diane marched to the lever and threw her palm against it. Her hand shook from the migration of the metal grip.

"No! Don't!" Arthur screamed, leaping to his feet.

Before he could gain any ground, Lloyd rushed him, landing a punch in his right eye to match the bruise on his left.

Diane yanked against the lever, surprised by the amount of resistance. The image of the brown-haired girl with an eye missing flashed through Diane's mind, recreating the ghastly scene of the hatchet in the poor girl's back, her arms flailing against the gravel path.

Diane knew she'd have a similar fate if she didn't manage to pull the damn lever back.

With another heave, the lever relented, just a quarter of the way down.

"Oh shit!" Lloyd screamed.

Diane whipped her chin over her shoulder. The seven-foot man's head stuck sideways through the cosmic doorway like a child peeking around a corner. The clay mask on his face cast shadows in his eyes—deep, hollow pits that lacked any semblance of humanity—but, somehow, Diane could feel his eyes on her.

Diane watched as his full form took shape through the black mass in the wall. His arms. His chest. A leg.

With two hands on the lever, she dropped all of her weight, successfully turning the lever down.

The black doorway disappeared in an instant, the basement wall having filled in around the madman's calf, trapping him in place.

Lloyd pulled her back before she could question it any further, leading her up the basement stairs. He stammered, "I stabbed him. I—I stabbed him through the arm, and he didn't even flinch. I don't—We—We have to—"

Sure enough, Lloyd's knife was stuck in the madman's forearm, the blade having gone clean through the flesh—in one end and out the other. With his other hand, the madman ripped the knife out. A *slush* of wet muscle and skin ripped through the basement, without even a hint of a whimper to accompany it.

Lloyd pulled Diane out of her stupor. "Come on!" he yelled.

They darted through the basement door and back into the living room.

That rancid smell hit Diane again, further reinforcing that something was very dead in the house.

Lloyd, heaving from the stench, ran through the living room and toward the front door. Diane ripped her arm away from him, her wits having returned to her, and followed behind.

"It's closed!" Lloyd yelled before flopping against the front door and thumbing for a deadbolt that wasn't there. "Did he lock it?! When could he have—I think I can kick it down!"

Thump! Lloyd attempted and failed to jar the front door open with his heel.

Diane turned to eye the path from which they'd just come. Past the closed basement door was a kitchen.

There had to be a back exit. She had to move fast before the madman ripped his leg free and came after them. Any moment now, the basement door would fly open and block their path.

Diane sprinted through the living room, eyes moving from the kitchen to the basement door. She was nearly past it when the door flung open, catching her foot. Muscle memory from her tumbling classes kicked in. She tucked her chin and rolled her spine along the floor, then shifted her weight to her feet, carrying her momentum forward and into the kitchen.

The stench was stronger now, and she knew why as soon as her eyes befell the island, the counters, the sink. Blood and fleshy chunks of viscera darkened the marble and stainless-steel surfaces like the back room of a butcher shop.

Diane gagged, fighting back the warm, sour bile climbing up her throat.

She refocused her eyes toward the end of the kitchen where a backdoor offered her a chance to escape. She lunged for the knob and turned it.

To her surprise, it opened with ease.

Diane descended three brick steps and gazed upon a black steel fence twice her height surrounding the backyard and bathed in the red glow of the sky, the thin rods looking like bloodied stakes.

The slim quarter of a blood moon hovered past the tall trees ominously in a crescent shape.

Unkempt grass tickled her bare legs as she stood. She couldn't jump the fence. She'd slap and scrape at it endlessly, giving the madman ample time to snatch her away.

"Help!" she wailed, her throat becoming instantly hoarse. "Help us!"

A series of screams erupted from inside the house—Lloyd begging and crying like an animal being led to slaughter.

Diane's eyes landed on a tree stump with an axe sticking out of it and piles of chopped wood on either side.

She ran to the stump, gripped the handle with both

hands, and pulled, unable to force it out, struggling just as she had with the metal lever.

Not again.

The backdoor came open behind her, succumbing to Lloyd's limp weight as he stumbled onto the steps with deep cuts running across his face and chest. He held his stomach with one hand, covering the wound that was now ripped into a larger gash, failing to keep the wet contents of his stomach inside. His other arm dangled with the elbow bent backward.

Lloyd fell to the grass, wailing in pain.

Diane shimmied the handle up and down like a see-saw, moving her eyes from the axe head to the mad-man as he stepped slowly down the stairs, looming over Lloyd as he clawed handfuls of grass with his one good hand.

The madman reached down to Lloyd's bad arm, forcing a squeal from the boy with his grip, and turned him onto his back.

Diane yanked at the axe—up, down, up, down—furiously loosening it from the stump.

The madman stomped his massive boot onto Lloyd's right kneecap, crushing it like a pumpkin. Lloyd's howls echoed through the trees, raspy and violent in a way that should have alerted the entirety of Love Lake.

Someone would have heard.

Someone would come for them.

Right?

With another helpless gasp of Lloyd's cries, the tears Diane had been holding back finally cascaded down her cheeks.

One final yank and the axe was free.

CRUNCH—The madman's boot came down on Lloyd's left kneecap. Diane could only hope the boy would pass out from shock.

She gripped her fingers tightly around the handle of the axe, knowing good and well that she'd be next if she didn't put the sharpened metal into the giant man now.

Diane rushed forward. With her teeth clenched and eyes bulging, she plunged the axe head into the man's midsection. She anticipated him clutching his gut, rounding over, falling to the ground.

But he had no reaction.

The man lowered his head to Diane, his dark eyes hidden behind the clay mask, as the wooden handle of the axe wobbled in place, seemingly more at home in the man's stomach than wedged into the tree stump.

The madman raised Lloyd's knife slowly, the blade catching a glimmer of the red sky above.

"Run!" Lloyd gurgled as blood erupted from his mouth and splattered against Diane's shin.

Diane turned and sprinted to the fence—truly her last resort.

As soon as she touched the steel, a shock ran through her body, turning her entire world black.

Diane awoke to Lloyd's dead eyes. The handle of his switchblade stood erect in his chest, surrounded by dried blood, and a line of black powder lay along his opened, bloody stomach.

As Diane followed the black line along the floorboards, she realized it was on her as well.

That smell ...

Algae and pond water.

A rapid *lap, lap, lap,* reverberated below the boards she lay against. Water sprung up through between the cracks, tickling her back.

Diane peered around the wooden structure surrounding her. A large A-frame ceiling, cobwebs and candles all around, with windows welcoming the stark light of the blood moon.

"Exteliotus... Magnafeelee... Atonatem..." A weathered voice spat some strange, foreign language Diane had never heard.

She rolled slowly to her side.

Past Lloyd, three other bodies filled her vision. One boy wore a tank top that was slashed diagonally down his chest. A boy in a windbreaker with a torn sleeve lay next to him, with his arm ripped off at the elbow. The brown-haired girl with her eye removed lay next to him on her side, the hatchet still stuck in her back.

Human beings reduced to meat puppets.

Waves of candlelight danced on their corpses, competing with the light of the blood moon and creating the unsettling illusion of animation. The powder lay atop all of them, connecting each body in a circle.

The madman stood with his back turned to Diane, head down and hands raised, his nonsensical words coarse like a pencil being sharpened. It took Diane a moment to realize that the wood plank hanging by his side was actually the handle of the axe still lodged in his gut. Diane began to think that he wasn't a man at all.

That he was some *thing*.

Then, she remembered him pulling the knife out of his forearm as if it had been stored there for safekeeping.

Diane stood slowly, nearly slipping on the wet boards, as the madman spoke into an opening in the floorboards—the empty half of the boathouse reserved for the boat. The unoccupied water bubbled and popped and sloshed onto the wood like the angry waves of a storm.

A cone of red light brightened from the swirling pool at the madman's feet. As his voice grew louder, the hue of the light deepened, casting a spotlight on the ceiling. Diane took careful, frightened steps forward and gazed into the hole in the water as it grew. She wanted so badly to close her eyes and fall asleep, to will herself into the comfort of her mattress back home and convince herself it was all a dream, but she couldn't look away.

The deep hum of a horn erupted from within the whirlpool, cracking her eardrums.

At the far edge of the whirlpool—that uncanny opening to the lake—a glistening, bulky, white intestine-like thing wiggled into view, rising up toward the madman. The long tendril appeared to have the thin skin of a sausage link, with fleshy white insides that moved separate from its exterior. It made contact with the man's leg, slithering around his body while the man stayed perfectly still, wrapping and sliding around the fabric as if exploring that portion of the man's body.

The tip of the thin, slimy, spineless thing then touched down on the floor beneath the man's leg, bringing the rest of its body squirming to the floor as well, having collected a coat of blood from the madman on its moist exterior. There were no eyes, no discernable features, and so Diane knew it couldn't see her horrified face, couldn't hear her broken breathing keeping pace with the drum of her heart.

She looked back toward the end of the boathouse, where the double doors she'd seen from the other side just minutes ago stood latched together.

The worm-like creature glided over the boy in the tank top's ankle and stopped.

A round nub forced its way through the skin at its front, revealing a vertical slit. What Diane could only comprehend as tiny worms seeped out of the slit, dropping along the boards next to the boy's leg.

One by one, the worms fell.

Plop ...

Plop ...

Plop ...

And one by one, they squirmed to life, rolling, flipping, sliding.

Having ejected a half-dozen smaller worms, the creature deflated, sinking into its own thin skin.

Whatthefuckwhatthefuckwhatthefuck, Diane repeated in her head.

She took a step back.

One of the worms moved up the boy's leg ...

Up his stomach ...

And into his ear.

Diane took another step back.

The board *creaked* under her weight.

She froze.

But nothing in the room responded to the sound. The madman remained motionless. The tiny worms continued their aimless pursuit. The large worm lay shriveled and dead on Tank Top's foot.

Suddenly, Tank Top gasped and sat upright quickly, looking into the glowing void at the madman's feet.

The dead boy turned his head to Diane, the strange

impression of a smile clinging to his face. His eyes were too wide, his cheeks too high, and without parting his teeth, the boy said, "You're supposed to be dead like this one."

Whatthefuckwhatthefuckwhatthefuck …

A worm slid toward Diane, inching closer fast. She imagined it crawling and entering her body, just like the worm had with Tank Top.

She smashed it with her sneaker, rubbing it into the floor to make sure every pasty little inch of it was spread thin.

"No!" Tank Top screamed.

Diane took long strides to the double doors, zoning in on the latch holding them together.

Her stomach dropped at the sight of a padlock holding the latch in place.

"Goddammit!" she screamed.

She turned, readying her hands to slap, claw, and punch her way out, even if she had to throw herself through a window to do so.

Tank Top brought himself to his feet with blood spilling out from the opening in his midsection. He marched awkwardly, unphased by the wound.

The one-eyed girl rose behind him, taking a long breath as if awakening from a deep sleep.

On the far side of the circle, the boy in the windbreaker rose as well, staring in amusement at the stump of his arm.

As her brain tried to make sense of the scene around her, Diane looked at Lloyd, wondering if he would soon rise with the same glazed stare she saw from the dead boy walking toward her like a puppet on strings, his limbs moving up and down in jittery movements as if being piloted by some other force.

"You killed one of us," Tank Top said, then formed an exaggerated frown. "We are sad."

Diane needed a weapon to bust down the door.

The axe hanging from the madman's midsection seemed good enough, as long as he stayed still.

She thrust her hands into Tank Top's chest, launching him backward and signaling a combination of a thud and a squashed bug as his head split open.

He laughed.

Windbreaker and the one-eyed girl stood before Diane, blocking her pathway to the madman. Diane grabbed a fixture of candles and threw it to the floor in front of them. The two corpses stared at the candles curiously as the flames met the wet floorboards and fizzled out.

Shit. Diane immediately felt stupid for thinking that would work.

The can of pepper spray scratched against her bare skin. The not-too-distant words of Lloyd reminded her of the dangers of using it with the open flames back inside the house. She glanced over at another candle fixture.

It was worth a shot.

With Windbreaker only inches away, Diane grabbed a candle off the fixture, ripped the pepper spray off her uniform, and pressed down hard, shooting the liquid through the flame.

A line of fire formed at the other side of the candle, clinging to Windbreaker's face. By the time Diane released the button, the entirety of the boy's forehead and hairline had caught fire.

Windbreaker kneeled, gasping excitedly; he looked up at Diane just before the fire spread to his eyes. "Is this pain?" the boy asked. "It's … wonderful." He laughed as the putrid stench of boiling skin reached inside Diane's nostrils.

Whatever remained in her stomach evacuated, landing with a *splat* on the floor.

"I would very much like to experience killing," the one-eyed girl said with the one good eye focused on Diane. This was the same girl who'd just be running for her life, screaming for someone—anyone—to save her.

Diane *had* to convince herself that that girl was long gone. She died. And whatever Diane did now, she'd be doing it to some monstrosity that *wasn't* that person.

Wasn't even a person at all.

The one-eye girl put her index finger in the empty socket, running it around the rim and making a churning, squishing sound. She panted joyfully as she removed her finger from the socket, bringing with a sticky glob of blood and puss.

Diane dodged the girl, tight-roped to the edge of the whirlpool, and ripped the axe from the madman's stomach, bringing wet chunks of viscera with it. He didn't move. Didn't flinch. Didn't make a sound.

The one-eyed girl sprang in front of Diane, arms

raised and fingers spread childishly, half her smile covered with a fresh coat of gore from the eye socket. "Killing!" she yelled.

Diane swung the axe and caught the girl's good eye, causing it to pop and spray viscous white matter. The girl fell to the ground. Diane stepped on her neck and yanked the axe free. The girl's arms flailed wildly. "It appears ... I—I can no longer see."

Diane stepped over the body, careful to dodge the waving arms. The burning boy continued to laugh, and Diane wondered how much longer the body would remain intact. Would the worm have to boil inside his head before the body failed?

She stepped around Lloyd's still corpse, hoping at least *he* could rest in peace, unlike the others, whose bodies had become playthings to some otherworldly force.

Tank Top stood in front of the wooden doors with his hand raised. "You cannot leave."

Without hesitation, Diane buried the axe in his chest, then grabbed the handle, wrestled him to the ground, and dragged him across the floor in an attempt to rip the axe out of his flesh.

She finally got the axe free, then swung down hard at his throat, partially separating his head from his shoulders with a sudden geyser of arterial spray that spurted up into Diane's face.

She wiped the blood from her eyes, gripped the axe again, and turned her attention to the double doors. She hacked away at the wood beside the lock, looking back after each chop and catching glimpses of the one-eyed girl prone with her arms waving and Windbreaker going still, then falling, finally cooked through. The flame fizzled out against the floorboards.

With one final hack, the latch separated from the wood.

Diane pulled the doors open, gazing out into the red-soaked land separating her from the lakehouse, a gravel road that forked into a driveway that would lead to her salvation, and no goddamn force field to stop her from leaving.

Diane was free.

She ascended the gravel driveway as fast as she could, still gripping the axe and concentrating on her footing, careful not to rush and stumble.

The unwelcome sight of Arthur standing in the doorway of the lakehouse with his hands raised encouraged her to clutch the axe even harder. He wasn't stopping her. Not now.

Diane was wearing three people's blood.

She'd make it four if she had to.

"Is it done?" Arthur asked.

Diane marched forward, watching as the red glow against his face revealed the realization that the ritual in question hadn't been successful. Not completely.

"Oh, god," Arthur said. "You're still you ... "

"I thought you didn't know what was going to happen, Arthur?"

"I—I'm sorry. My family ... We need the money ... Fuck this." He sprinted into the gravel driveway.

Just as she was about to sprint after him, a scream halted her.

"Diane!"

It couldn't have been him.

"Diane, I'm hurt!" Lloyd cried out. Suddenly, the axe was heavier in her hands.

Lloyd rolled out of the double doors like an infant learning to walk. With his cheek pressed against the gravel, his eyes caught Diane.

"Die," he said, then pressed his bent-back arm to the ground, pushing himself up. Bones *cracked* as the twisted arm bore weight. "Die ... please help." He wiggled one leg—crooked from his crushed kneecap—to the side, eyeing it in amusement, then put weight on his foot, bringing his torso up. His other mangled leg swung to his side, and he began walking toward her, his torso parallel to the ground, crawling like a spider as his tendons snapped and bones refused to adjust to their new structure.

"Die," he said, "let's go to the party .... Ar—Ar—Arthur's party. Would you l—like to go?" Lloyd's limbs popped, his joints sloshing in his skin, his hands and feet dragging along the gravel.

"What are you?" Diane stood with the axe ready in her hands and the thing came closer.

"Your ... b—boyfriend. Lloyd ... is my name."

"You're not him. What ... are you?"

In an attempt to stand, the thing that used to be Lloyd leaned back on its calves and his legs folded back with a wet *CRUNCH*. The corpse's stomach fell to its toes. It pressed itself up and looked at Diane with confused eyes.

"We live among the stars," it said, "in a dimension beyond your world, devoid of the rules that govern time and space. There is nothing. An infinite nothing. We only want to feel. We want to live as you do. To experience y—your ... biological sensations." The thing clutched Diane's skirt. "Will you a—allow me ... to feel?"

Another tear ran down Diane's cheek as she smashed the axe into Lloyd's skull.

PRESENT DAY

Freaky Local Legends Podcasts:

The Blood Moon Murders

(Transcript)

Police would search the grounds of the lake house later that morning. They found the bodies of the victims—one burned, one decapitated, and, well … we already mentioned the boyfriend. Diane's initial claim of a worm monster, well … It wasn't there. Her story changed quickly after that, claiming she had stress-induced hallucinations.

Wendy Gibbs, the young lady with one eye gouged out and the other hacked clean through, actually survived. But, if you know this story well enough, you'll know she died shortly thereafter from what coroners could only determine to be … decay.

Very strange, indeed.

Diane Doakes' statement indicated that Arthur Dodson had lured her and Lloyd to Love Lake, where a murderous psychopath dragged their bodies to the boathouse to perform a satanic ritual, which wasn't outside the realm of possibility in the public consciousness. This was the 80s, after all. She didn't admit to killing any of the kids, despite having their blood all over her.

After a lengthy psych evaluation and Wendy Gibbs' statement that cleared her of any wrongdoing, she was released. In fact, before she passed away, Wendy said that Diane *helped* her.

Arthur Dodson, by all accounts, was never there. An air-tight alibi placed him on the other side of town, and a mysterious hotshot lawyer saw to it that nobody ever questioned Arthur's whereabouts that night ever again.

What about that old-money family who owned the lake house? No one knows *exactly* who they are, but if we're taking Diane's original account of the events before she changed her story, the tin foil hat on my dresser is telling me that maybe … just maybe … that family came to Arthur's rescue to keep things quiet.

They couldn't protect him for long, though. Arthur Dodson was killed in his home fifteen years later. One shot to the head. The bullet was removed by the shooter.

I'm sure you have a lot of questions, as do I. The one that occupies my mind most prominently is … Why was the blood moon so important to the ritual? You may be wondering why I chose to do this episode now. Well, the next blood moon will occur again in Echo Ridge within two weeks' time. Currently, Diane Doakes lives in seclusion with a stockpile of guns and ammunition on the outskirts of town, and part of me wonders if the Echo Ridge Giant is still out there, waiting on the next blood moon to reign terror on the community again.

As a firm believer in things outside our current understanding of reality, I, for one, am hoping Diane is counting down the days for a rematch.

Until next week, my friends … stay freaky.

THE END

Upcoming Adult Titles From Mad Axe Media

Additional Information on these titles can be found at
www.madaxemedia.com

Readings From Cursed Room 301
Edited by Joey Powell
July 2024

An anthology of twisted horror genre tropes featuring Patrick Barb, Chloe Spencer, Briana Morgan, Steph Nelson, Alyson Hasson, Jason A. Jones, Alex Hunter, Caleb James K., Nadine Stewart, AudraKate Gonzalez, Josh Powell, Matt Carlin, David Royce, Spencer Hamilton, Nikki Kossaris, and Isaac Nightingale.

Professor Douglas Primm has been called in to teach a horror writing class at Bloodworth College in Room 301, a lecture hall rumored to be cursed. His only responsibility for the next week is to read aloud the works submitted by his students for the prompt "Horror Genre Tropes".

As Primm reads these tales aloud, they become increasingly unhinged, as does his grip on reality, causing him to wonder whether he too may be succumbing to the dark hold of Room 301.

And perhaps the students who inhabit it...

Hiding Lies
By Stephanie Rose
October 2024

"I still remember standing outside the blazing house. I wasn't sorry."

Lydia Walker is a forensic photographer, trudging through life in the shadow of her traumatic past, when she is assigned a case centered around the gruesome murder of a camping couple. Her personal life begins to improve after a chance encounter that makes her feel like she's finally connected with someone, a fellow tortured soul named Adam.

As more victims are unearthed, she discovers she has a personal connection to the case that causes her commitment to grow while keeping her motives opaque to her colleagues.

Will she sacrifice her reputation and her morality to explore her darker urges?

Or will she uphold the justice system that failed her?

JK-LOL
By Patrick Barb
January 2025

Ted Hideman is a family man and a renowned tech start up guru.

He's also the notorious impossible-to-track online troll JK-LOL.

When his online persona spills over into the real world, attacking those he's virtually harassed and leaving a trail of bodies from California to Mississippi, the disgraced Silicon Valley wünderkind must abandon the protective anonymity of the online sphere and desperately search for answers in the real world.

Following in the tradition of *Black Mirror* and Barb's sci-fi/horror novelette *Helicopter Parenting in the Age of Drone Warfare*, *JK-LOL* highlights the dark side of tech and how terrifying connectivity can truly be.

Unholy
By J.V. Gachs
March 2025

Magdalena, a forty-eight-year-old cloistered nun, has two days to stop the Apocalypse.

After she recruits Ana, a sex shop owner and domestic violence survivor, the duo set out to infiltrate the sex cult that will host the Antichrist' birth. Magdalena's faith and determination are put to the test as she embraces her more sinful and sexual needs during the infiltration and second-guesses her childhood encounter with an archangel.

J.V. Gachs, author of *Epiphany*, brings her signature brand of religious horror to a story that blends *Eyes Wide Shut* with devil smut.

Son of a Serial Killer
By Andrew Adams
May 2025

Glen Overton is a thirty-year-old corporate data clerk and he hates every second of it. Having never known his father, his alcoholic mother lets slip one night that he is the son of one of the most uber infamous serial killers, Brock Blackwood, who stirred up a media storm back in the 70s and 80s.

When word gets out, Brock's old superfans rush forward to support Glen, while others who vividly remember the horrors want him gone immediately, with or without force. Glen must come to terms with who he truly is and navigate pressure from all angles to either walk in his father's shadow or break free from it for good.

ADVANCE PRAISE FOR

Hiding Lies
By Stephanie Rose

"I read the whole thing eyes covered and jaw dropped. Rose exposes every dark aspect of humanity swiftly and unapologetically and gives us the scariest duo I've seen in fiction yet!"

-CJ Leede, author of *Maeve Fly*

"There is a darkness at the core of *Hiding Lies* that seeps out from its pages, thicker than blood, as pitch black as the Portland woods at midnight. One can't help but feel as though it stains their fingers, their eyes, their very soul. Tread carefully through this brutal book. It marks you."

-Clay McLeod Chapman, author of *What Kind of Mother* and *Ghost Eaters*

"Stephanie Rose has come out of hiding with this undeniably thrilling debut. A disturbing cat and mouse tale with the ferocity of your favorite Hannibal episode, *Hiding Lies* will set up camp in the shadows of your psyche long after the final breathtaking page is turned."

-Brian McAuley, author of *Candy Cain Kills* and *Curse of the Reaper*

"Dark, disturbing, and twisty ... What more could you want from a serial killer novel? Stephanie Rose's debut novel is a wicked cat-and-mouse game that will keep you up late reading ... and maybe looking over your shoulder."

-Samantha Downing, internationally bestselling author of *My Lovely Wife*

ADVANCE PRAISE FOR

JK-LOL
By Patrick Barb

"Told in an engaging format, and as crudely funny as it is horrifically sinister, *JK-LOL* is a thrilling ride from start to finish, one that will force you to question your understanding of online anonymity and the pervasiveness of Internet bigotry."

-Chloe Spencer, author of *Mewing* and *Monstersona*

"Patrick Barb has proven that he knows how to deliver a gut punch of a story, and *JK-LOL* is absolutely that. This book is disturbing in all the right ways. I couldn't look away, and thanks to Barb's razor-sharp prose and relatable characters, I absolutely didn't want to."

-Steph Nelson, author of *The Vein* and *The Final Scene*

"I flew through this fast-paced, action-packed commentary on society's inseparable integration with online spaces and the ominous anonymity that many seemingly normal people hide behind, allowing them to live a sadistic secret life. Full of twists, with plenty of visceral gory scenes throughout, this is just the quick, smart, and transgressive read so many are looking for."

-Emma E. Murray, author of *Crushing Snails*

Upcoming Totally Freaked! Young Adult Titles From Mad Axe Media

Standalone spooky tales of 90s-set horror!
Additional Information on these titles can be found at
www.madaxemedia.com

A Mall-ignant Christmas
By Damien Casey
December 2024

Bayfield, Ohio... Christmas Eve, 1995
A teenage girl named Millie Lisa goes missing while Christmas shopping for her father. Her last known whereabouts? A golf store in a mall.

Now...
A paranormal research team discovers a secret floor of their local mall trapped in the year 1995 during the holiday season. The team sets out to create the latest viral paranormal video. What will they find? A giant gingerbread man? An ancient Christmas legend? Or maybe...

They'll discover what really happened to Millie Lisa.

Birthday Party Demon
By Wendy Dalrymple
February 2025

BFFs Tina, Eve, and Lacey come together for a Sweet 16 slumber party that goes sideways when they accidentally summon more than a good time. After Lacey becomes possessed and traps her friends in a fashion catalog, Tina and Eve must find their way out of a totally fabulous new world before the demon overtakes Lacey's body completely.

CodeSkull
By Chloe Spencer
July 2025

An ambitious arcade gamer, Mick, is gifted a CD of an RPG game by her rival, Tommy. But when she plays it, she inadvertently unleashes a terrifying technological creature that can infest and overload any electrically powered object. After their classmate meets a grisly end, the two must team up in order to save their small town—and possibly the world—from annihilation.

Coffin Corner
By T.T. Madden
October 2025

Inspired by creepypastas and analog horrors, Coffin Corner follows a group of high schoolers on Halloween night as they enter the fabled Gorman's House, a traveling haunted attraction that's so scary no one has ever completed it. But they soon discover this haunted attraction contains real supernatural frights.

A Night in Echo Ridge Park
By A.L. Davidson
November 2025

A plucky park ranger and a grumpy hunter find themselves lost in the wilderness as some seriously strange things begin happening in the forest. Mushroom men, pulsating green lights, and disembodied whistling drive them deeper and deeper into the woods, and their only hope of surviving the night rests within the mysterious radio tower in the mountains.

You Love Horror
We Love Horror Storytelling

@MADAXEMEDIA

MADAXEMEDIA.COM

Keep it Weird